Disney

MICKEY MOUSE & FRIENDS

pi kids

publications international, ltd.

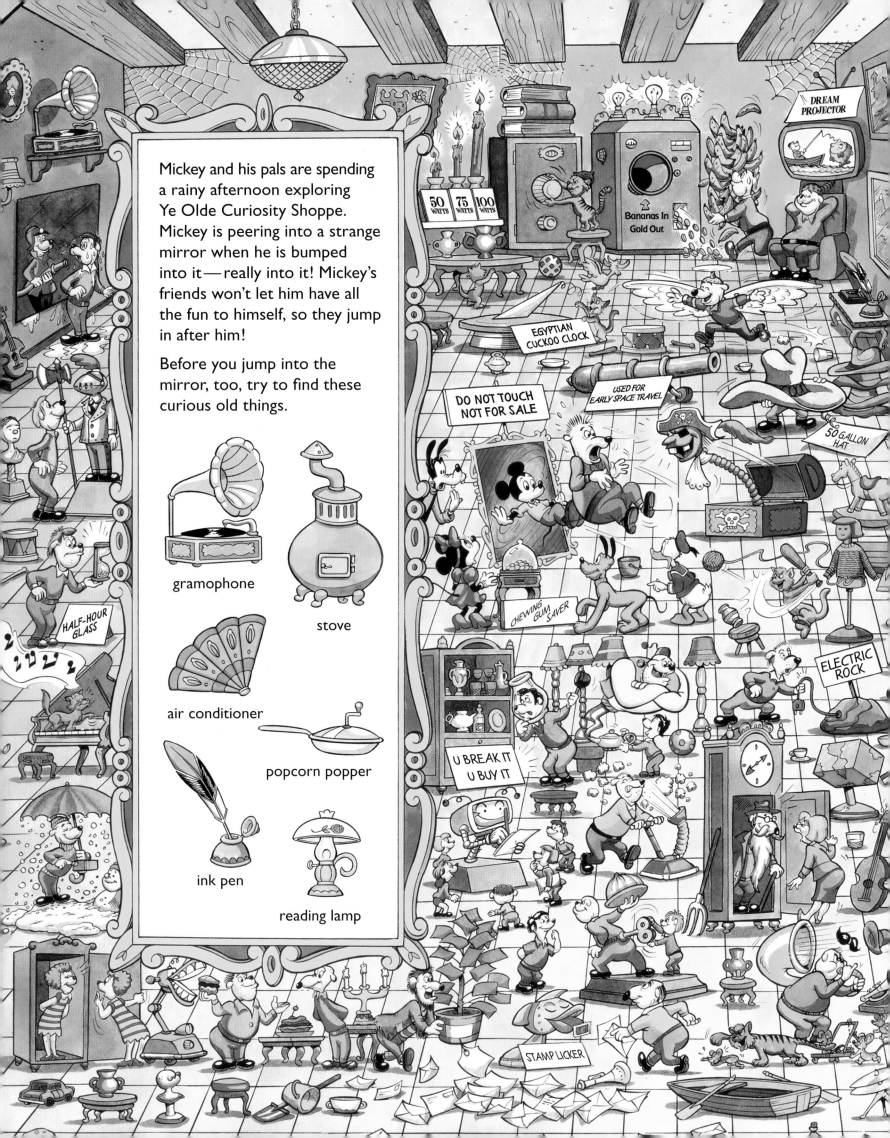

Mickey and his pals are spending a rainy afternoon exploring Ye Olde Curiosity Shoppe. Mickey is peering into a strange mirror when he is bumped into it—really into it! Mickey's friends won't let him have all the fun to himself, so they jump in after him!

Before you jump into the mirror, too, try to find these curious old things.

gramophone

stove

air conditioner

popcorn popper

ink pen

reading lamp

It's the year 2999, and Robo-Pete is cloning hundreds of naughty Mickeys, Minnies, Goofys, Donalds, and Plutos!

First, find the remote to turn off the Robo-Clone Machine. Then help the gang look for these Robo-Clones.

remote

Sprocket Mickey

Gyro Goofy

Submarine Donald

Rocket Minnie

Spring-Action Pluto

Next stop: Main Street, USA! The Saturday matinee just ended, and everyone is talking about the new movie, *Aliens from the Pistachio Planet*. Or *was* it a movie?

Good thing Mickey and his pals are on the scene to send these real space aliens home!

Can you find aliens in these flavors?

orange

french vanilla

Neapolitan

mint chip

chocolate

peppermint

strawberry

Ahoy! Mickey is about to take a saltwater bath. Can his friends rescue him from his perilous perch? Or will Patch-Eye Pete and his scurvy seadogs make him walk off the plank?

It's easy to spot Mickey, but can you find these pirates?

Slippery Sam

Bilge-Water Betsy

Hard-Headed Harry

Jolly Roger

Pretty-Boy Lloyd

Cue-Ball Bob

Peg-Leg Peg

CASTAWAYS CHARTER CO.

Neptune Snacks Cove

WANTED

Come one, come all to see noble Sir Mickey match jousting skills with Sir Foulplay, the dreaded Knight of Cheatham!

Can you find these silly knights in Merrie Olde England?

Knight of the Kitchen Table

Knight of the Changing Table

Knight of the Round Table

Knight of the Tea Party Table

Knight of the Pool Table

Knight of the Multiplication Table

Spells Broken by Merlin

Ye Ox of Oxford vs. Goofy the Unfortunate

Draw Bridge

Rockin' Robin

Rockin' Robin and his Merrie Five

I Love Little John

TAXES

Mickey and the gang hop through the mirror again for a change of scenery. The Stone Age is lovely to look at, but not much is happening. Ugh! To get things "rocking," Mickey suggests a talent show.

Can you find these talented performers?

Ugga

Oop

Grunt

Oona

Eeeg

Gorp

When in Rome, do as the Romans do! That's Mickey's advice to his pals when they find themselves at Caesar's place. The gang is trying to blend in, but it's all Greek to them!

Can you find these Roman things?

XV
Roman numeral

this soldier

goddess

toga

key

bathtub

Roman candle

MARCH
XV

PORTRAITS WHILE YOU WAIT

Three cheers for Mickey, Minnie, Donald, Goofy, and Pluto! Their travels through time have made them heroes.

Can you find some travelers who have slipped through the mirror and followed Mickey home?

robot

cowboy

alien

pirate

caveman

Roman

knight

Go back to Ye Olde Curiosity Shoppe to find curious cats doing these things.

- ❒ Wearing a hat
- ❒ Fishing in a fishbowl
- ❒ Painting a picture
- ❒ Catching a mouse
- ❒ Playing the piano
- ❒ Cracking a safe
- ❒ Reading a book
- ❒ Unknitting a sweater

Pardner, git on back to Dry Gulch to find these things from the wild west.

- ❒ A horse thief
- ❒ A ten-gallon hat
- ❒ A rattlesnake
- ❒ A cow puncher
- ❒ Chief Standing Cow
- ❒ A mail-order bride

Go back to the future. Can you find these robo-citizens?

- ❒ A robo-cop
- ❒ A robo-doctor
- ❒ A robo-chef
- ❒ A robo-dogcatcher
- ❒ A robo-ballerina
- ❒ A robo-tennis player

Rock 'n' roll back to Main Street, USA! Can you find these nifty Fifties things?

- ❒ A poodle in a skirt
- ❒ A hula hoop
- ❒ A sock hopping
- ❒ A real beehive hairdo
- ❒ A jukebox
- ❒ Saddle shoes
- ❒ A rock and roll